Water

and Discovering Japan

By Bret Easton Ellis

Glamorama

The Informers

American Psycho

The Rules of Attraction

Less Than Zero

Lunar Park

Bret Easton Ellis

Water from the Sun and Discovering Japan

PICADOR SHOTS

First published 2006 by Picador
an imprint of Pan Macmillan Ltd
Pan Macmillan, 20 New Wharf Road, London N1 9RR
Basingstoke and Oxford
Associated companies throughout the world
www.panmacmillan.com

ISBN-13: 978-0-330-44582-5
ISBN-10: 0-330-44582-0

1 3 5 7 9 8 6 4 2

A CIP catalogue record for this book is available from the British Library.

Typeset by Intype Libra Ltd
Printed and bound in Great Britain by
Mackays of Chatham plc, Chatham, Kent

Water from the Sun

DANNY IS ON MY bed and depressed because Ricky was picked up by a break-dancer at the Odyssey on the night of the Duran Duran look-alike contest and murdered. It seems that Biff, Ricky's current lover, called Danny after getting my number from someone at the station and told him the news. I walk in and all Danny says is "Ricky's dead. Throat slit. All of his blood drained from his body. Biff called." Danny doesn't move or explain the tone in which Biff relayed this news and he doesn't take off the Wayfarer sunglasses he's wearing even though he's inside and it's almost eight. He just lies there watching some religious show on cable and I don't know what to say.

I'm just relieved that he's still here, that he hasn't left.

Now, in the bathroom, unbuttoning my blouse, unzipping my skirt, I call out, "Did you tape the newscast?"

"No," Danny says.

"Why not?" I ask, pausing before putting on a robe.

"Wanted to tape 'The Jetsons,'" he says dully.

I don't say anything coming out of the bathroom. I walk over to the bed. Danny is wearing a pair of khaki shorts and a FOOTLOOSE T-shirt he got the night of the premiere party at the studio his father is executive in charge of production at. I look down at him, see my reflection, distorted, warped, in the lenses of the sunglasses, and then, carrying my blouse and skirt, walk into the closet and toss them into a hamper. I close the closet door, stand over the bed.

"Move over," I tell him.

He doesn't move over, just lies there. "Ricky's

dead. All of his blood drained out of him. He looked black. Biff called," he says again, coldly.

"And I thought I told you to keep the phone off the hook or unplug it or something," I say, sitting down anyway. "I thought I told you that I'll take all my calls at the station."

"Ricky's dead," Danny mutters.

"Someone snapped off my windshield wipers today, for some reason," I say after a while, taking the control box from him and changing the channel. "They left a note. It said 'Mi hermana.'"

"Biff," he sighs, and then, "What did you do? Rip off a Taco Bell?"

"Biff snapped off my windshield wipers?"

Nothing.

"Why didn't you tape the newscast tonight?" I ask softly, trying not to press too hard.

"Because Ricky's dead."

"But you taped 'The Jeffersons,'" I say accusingly, trying not to lose patience. I turn the channel to MTV, a lame attempt to please him. Unfortunately, a Duran Duran video is on.

"'The Jetsons,'" he says. "Not 'The Jeffersons.' I taped 'The Jetsons.' Turn that *off*."

"But you always tape the newscasts," I'm whining, trying not to. "You know I like to watch them." Pause. "I thought you've seen all 'The Jetsons.'"

Danny doesn't say anything, just recrosses long, sculpted legs.

"And what was the phone doing on the hook?" I ask, trying to sound amused.

He gets up from the bed so suddenly that it startles me. He walks over to the glass doors that open onto the balcony and looks out over the canyons. It's light outside and warm and beyond Danny it's still possible to see heat rising up off the hills and then I'm saying "Just don't leave" and he says "I don't even know what I'm doing here" and I ask, almost dutifully, "Why are you here?" and he says "Because my father kicked me out of the house" and I ask "Why?" and Danny says "Because my father asked me 'Why don't you get a job?' and I said 'Why don't you suck my dick?'"

He pauses and, having read about Edward, I wonder if he actually did, but then Danny says, "I'm sick of having this conversation. We've had it too many times."

"We haven't even had it once," I say softly.

Danny turns away from the glass doors, leans against them and swallows hard, staring at a new video on MTV.

I look away from him, following his gaze to the TV screen. A young girl in a black bikini is being terrorized by three muscular, near-naked masked men, all playing guitars. The girl runs into a room and starts to claw at Venetian blinds as fog or smoke starts to pour into the room. The video ends, resolved in some way, and I turn back to look at Danny. He's still staring at the TV. A commercial for the Lost Weekend with Van Halen contest. David Lee Roth, looking stoned and with two sparsely dressed girls sitting on either side of him, leers into the camera and asks, "How about a little joyride in my limo?" I look back over at Danny.

"Just don't leave," I sigh, not caring if I sound pathetic.

"I signed up for that," he says, sunglasses still on.

I reach over, disconnecting the phone, and think about the window wipers being snapped off.

"So you signed up for the Lost Weekend contest?" I ask. "Is that what we were talking about?"

I'm having lunch with Sheldon in a restaurant on Melrose. It's noon and the restaurant is already crowded and quiet. Soft rock plays over a stereo system. Cool air drifts from three large slowly spinning silver fans hooked to the ceiling. Sheldon sips Perrier and I wait for his response. He sets down the large iced glass and looks out the window and actually stares at a palm tree, which I find momentarily distressing.

"Sheldon?" I say.

"Two weeks?" he asks.

"I'll take one if that's all you can get me." I'm looking at my plate: a huge, uneaten Caesar salad.

"What is this week for? Where are you going?" Sheldon seems actually concerned.

"I want to go somewhere." I shrug. "Just take some time off."

"Where?"

"Somewhere."

"Where is somewhere? Jesus, Cheryl."

"I don't know where somewhere is, Sheldon."

"Are you falling apart on me, baby?" Sheldon asks.

"What is this, Sheldon? What the fuck's going on? Can you get me the week off or not?" I pick up a spoon, stab at the salad, lift lettuce to my mouth. It falls off, back onto the plate. I put the spoon down. Sheldon looks at me, so bewildered that I have to turn away.

"You know, um, I'll try," Sheldon says soothingly, still stunned. "You know I'd do anything for you."

"You'll *try*?" I ask, incredulous.

"You lack faith. That's your problem," Sheldon says. "You lack faith. And you haven't joined a gym."

"My agent is telling me that *I* lack faith?" I ask. "My life must really be a disaster."

"You should work out." Sheldon sighs.

"I don't lack faith, Sheldon. I just need to go to Las Cruces for a week." I start to pick at the salad again, making sure Sheldon notices I've picked up a fork. "I used to work out," I mutter. "I used to work out all the time."

"I'll see what I can do. I'll talk to Jerry. And Jerry will talk to Evan. But you know what they say." Sheldon sighs, looking out at the palm tree. "Can't get water from the sun."

"What the hell are you talking about?" I say, then, "Are you on dope or something, Sheldon?"

The check comes and Sheldon pulls out his wallet and then a credit card.

"You still living with that pretty boy?" he asks with what sounds like definite disdain.

"I like him, Sheldon," I say and then, with less confidence, "He likes me."

"I'm sure. I'm sure he does, Cheryl," Sheldon says. "You didn't want dessert, did you?"

I shake my head, tempted, finally, to eat the rest of the unfinished salad, but the waiter comes and takes the plate away. Everyone in the restaurant, it feels, recognizes me.

"Turn that frown upside down," Sheldon says. He's putting his wallet back in his pocket.

"What would that get me—an upside-down frown, what?"

From the way Sheldon is looking at me, I try to smile and put my napkin on the table, mimicking a normal person.

"Your phone has been, um, busy lately," Sheldon mentions softly.

"You can get hold of me at the station," I say. "It doesn't mean anything."

"Talk to William lately?"

"I don't think I want to talk to William."

"I think he wants to talk to you."

"How do you know?"

"I've seen him a couple of times." Sheldon shrugs. "Around."

"Jesus," I'm saying. "I don't want to see that creep."

A young Mexican boy clears away our water glasses.

"Cheryl, most people I know will speak to their ex-husband if their ex-husband wants to speak to them. It's no biggie. What is this? You can't even talk to him on the phone?"

"He can get hold of me at the station," I say. "I don't want to talk to William. He's pathetic." I'm looking out the window again, at two teenage girls with short blond hair, wearing miniskirts, who are walking by with a tall blond boy and the boy reminds me of Danny. It isn't that the boy looks exactly like Danny—he does—it's more the apathetic shuffle, the way he checks himself out in the window of this restaurant, the same pair of Wayfarers. And for a moment he takes off his sunglasses and stares right at me even though he doesn't see me and his hand runs through short blondish hair and the two girls lean up against the palm tree Sheldon was staring at and light cigarettes and the boy puts his sunglasses back on and makes sure they are not crooked and turns away and walks down Melrose and the two girls leave the palm tree and follow the boy.

"Know him?" Sheldon asks.

William calls me at the station around three. I'm at my desk working on a story about the twentieth anniversary of the Kitty Genovese slaying when he calls. He tells me that my phone has been busy lately and that we should have dinner one night this week. I tell him that I've been busy, tired, that there's too much work to complete. William keeps mentioning the name of a new Italian restaurant on Sunset.

"What about Linda?" I realize I should not have said this, that it will give William the idea that I might be considering his offer. "She's in Palm Springs for a couple of days."

"What about Linda?"

"What about her?"

"What about Linda?"

"I think I've missed you."

I hang up the phone and stare at pictures of Kitty Genovese's body and William doesn't call back. In makeup, Simon talks about a screenplay he's working on about break-dancing in West Hollywood. Once the news begins I stare straight into the camera and hope that Danny is watching since it's really the only time he ever looks at me. I smile warmly before each commercial break even if it's grossly inappropriate and at the end of the broadcast I'm tempted to mouth "Good night, Danny." But at the Gelson's in Brentwood I see a badly burned little boy in a basket and I remember the way William said "I think I've missed you" right before I hung up on him and when I come out of the market the sky is light and too purple and still.

There is a white VW Rabbit parked next to Danny's red Porsche in the driveway, which is parked next to a giant tumbleweed. I drive past the cars and park my Jaguar in the carport and sit there for a long time before I get out and carry the bag of groceries inside. I set them on the kitchen table, then open the refrigerator and drink half a Tab. There is a note on the table from the maid, written in broken English, about William calling. I walk over to the phone, unplug it and crumple the note up. A boy, maybe nineteen, twenty, with short blond hair and tan, wearing only blue shorts and sandals, walks into the kitchen, stopping suddenly. We stare at each other for a moment.

"Uh, hello?" I say.

"Hi," the boy says, starting to smile.

"Who are you?"

"Um, I'm Biff. Hi."

"Biff?" I ask. "You're Biff?"

He begins to back out of the kitchen. around.”

ıd there with the note about William still cru.. ıed in my hand. I throw it away and walk up the stairs. The front door slams shut and I can hear the sound of the VW Rabbit starting, backing out of the driveway, moving down the street.

Danny is lying under a thin white sheet on my bed, staring at the television. Wadded-up pieces of Kleenex are scattered on the floor by the side of the bed, next to a deck of tarot cards and an avocado. It’s hot in the room and I open the balcony doors, then walk into the bathroom, change into my robe and move silently over to the Betamax and rewind the tape. I look over my shoulder at Danny, still staring at the TV screen I’m blocking. I press Play and a Beach Boys concert comes on. I fast-forward the tape and press Play. There isn’t anything on it except for the Beach Boys.

“You didn’t tape the newscast tonight?”

"Yeah. I did."

"But there's nothing there." I'm pointing at the Betamax.

"Really?" He sighs.

"There's nothing there."

Danny thinks about it a moment, then groans, "Oh man, I'm sorry. I had to tape the Beach Boys concert."

Pause, then, "You *had* to tape a Beach Boys concert?"

"It was the last concert before Brian Williams died," Danny says.

I sigh, drum my fingers on the Betamax. "It wasn't Brian Williams, you moron. It was Dennis Wilson."

"No, it wasn't," he says, sitting up a little. "It was Brian."

"You've missed taping the show two nights in a row now." I walk into the bathroom and turn on the faucets in the bathtub. "And it was Dennis," I call out.

"I don't know where the hell you heard that," I hear him say. "It was Brian."

"It was Dennis Wilson," I say loudly, bending down, feeling the water.

"No way. You're totally wrong. It was Brian," he says. He gets up from the bed with the sheet wrapped around him, grabs the remote control and lies back down.

"It was Dennis." I walk out of the bathroom.

"Brian," he says, turning the channel to MTV. "You are wrong to the max."

"It was Dennis, you little asshole," I scream at him as I leave the room and walk downstairs, flip on the air-conditioning and then, in the kitchen, open a bottle of white wine. I take a glass out of a cupboard and walk back upstairs.

"William called this afternoon," Danny says.

"What did you tell him?" I pour myself a glass of wine and sip it, trying to calm down.

"That we were dry humping and you couldn't make it to the phone," Danny says, grinning.

"Dry humping? So you weren't exactly lying."

"Right." He snorts.

"Why didn't you just leave the goddamned phone unplugged?" I scream at him.

"You're crazy." He sits up suddenly. "What is this shit about the phone? You're crazy, you're . . . you're . . ." He trails off, unable to find the right word.

"And what was that little surfer doing in my house?" I finish one glass of wine, a little nauseated, then pour another.

"That was Biff," Danny says defensively. "He doesn't surf."

"Well, he looked real upset," I say loudly, sarcastic, taking off my robe.

In the bathroom I ease myself into warm water, turn the faucets off, lie back, sipping the wine. Danny, with the sheet wrapped around him, walks in and throws Kleenex into the wastebasket and then wipes his hand on the sheet. He puts the toilet seat down and sits and lights a joint he's holding. I close my eyes, take a large swallow of wine. The only sounds: music coming from MTV, one of the faucets dripping, Danny sucking on a thinly rolled joint. I'm just noticing that sometime today Danny bleached his hair white.

"Want some weed?" he asks, coughing.

"What?" I ask.

"Some weed?" He holds the joint out to me.

"No," I'm saying. "No weed."

Danny sits back and I'm feeling self-conscious, so I roll over onto my stomach, but it's uncomfortable and I roll over onto my side and then onto my back but he's not looking at me anyway. His eyes are closed. He speaks.

In monotone: "Biff was down on Sunset today and he came to a stoplight and he told me he saw this old deformed woman with a totally big head and long puffy fat hands and she was, like, screaming and drooling, holding up traffic." He takes another hit off the joint, holds it in. "And she was naked." He exhales, then says, benignly, "She was at a bus stop way down on the Strip, maybe near Hillhurst." He takes another hit off the joint, holds it in.

I picture the image clearly and, after thinking about it, ask, "Why in the hell did you tell me that?"

He shrugs, doesn't say anything. He just opens his eyes and stares at the red tip of the joint and blows on it I reach over the side of the tub and pour another glass of wine.

"You tell *me* something," he finally says.

"Like, trade information?"

"Whatever."

"I . . . want a child?" I say, guessing.

After a long pause, Danny shrugs, says, "Bitchin'."

"Bitchin'?" I close my eyes and very evenly ask, "Did you just say bitchin'?"

"Don't mock me, man," he says, getting up, going over to the mirror. He scratches at an imaginary mark on his chin, turns away.

"It's no use," I say suddenly.

"I'm too young," he says. "Duh."

"I can't even remember when I met you," I say, quietly, then I look up at him.

"What?" he asks, surprised. "You expect me to remember?" He drops the sheet and, nude, walks back to the toilet and sits down and takes a swig from the bottle of white wine. I notice a scar on the inside of his thigh and I reach out and touch his leg. He pulls back, takes a drag on the joint. My hand stays there, in space, and I bring it back, embarrassed.

"Would a smart person make fun of me for asking you what you're thinking?"

"I have—" He stops, then slowly continues. "I have been thinking about how awful it was, losing my virginity." He pauses. "I have been thinking about that all day."

"It usually is when you lose it to a truck driver." A long, hateful pause. I turn away. "That was stupid." I want to touch him again but sip Chardonnay instead.

"What makes you so fucking perfect?" His eyes narrow, the jaw sets. He gets up, bends over, picks up the sheet, walks back into the bedroom. I get up out of the tub and dry off and, a little drunk, walk into the room, naked, holding the bottle of wine and my glass, and I get under the sheet with him. He turns channels. I do not know why he is here or where we met and he's lying next to me, naked, gazing at videos.

"Does your husband know about this?" he asks, a tone of false amusement. "He says the divorce isn't finalized. He says he's not your ex."

I don't move, don't answer, for a moment I don't see Danny or anything else in the room.

"Well?"

I need another glass of wine but I force myself to wait a few minutes before I pour it. Another video. Danny hums along with it. I remember sitting in a car in the parking lot of the Galleria and William holding my hand.

"Does it matter?" I say once the video ends. I close my eyes, easily pretend that I'm not here. When I open them it's darker in the room and I look over at Danny and he's still staring at the TV. A photograph of L.A. at night is on the screen.

A red streak flies over the neon landscape. The name of a local radio station appears.

"Do you like him?" Danny asks.

"No. I really don't." I sip the wine, easing toward tired. "Do you like . . . him?"

"Who? Your husband?"

"No," I say. "Biff, Boff, Buff, whatever."

"What?"

"Do you like him?" I ask again. "More than me?"

Danny doesn't say anything.

"You don't have to answer immediately." I could say this stronger but don't. "As if you're capable."

"Don't ask me this," he says, his eyes a dull gray-blue, blank, half closed. "Just don't ask me this. Don't do this."

"It's just all so typical." I'm giggling.

"What did Tarzan say when he saw the elephants coming over the hill?" he asks, yawning.

"What?" I'm still giggling, my eyes closed.

"Here come the elephants over the hill."

"I think I've heard this one before." I'm picturing Danny's long tan fingers and then, less appealing, where his tan line stops, starts again, the thick unsmiling lips.

"What did Tarzan say when he saw the elephants come over the hill with raincoats on?" he asks.

I finish the wine and set the glass on the nightstand, next to an empty bottle. "What?"

"Here come the elephants over the hill wearing raincoats." He waits for my response.

"He . . . did?" I ask, finally.

"What did Tarzan say when he saw the elephants come over the hill with sunglasses on?"

"I don't think I really want to know this, Danny," I say, my tongue thick, closing my eyes again, things clogged.

"Nothing," Danny says lifelessly. "He didn't recognize them."

"Why are you telling me this?"

"I don't know." Pause. "To keep me amused maybe."

"What?" I say, drifting. "What did you say?"

"To keep me amused?"

I fall asleep next to him for a minute, then wake up but don't open my eyes. My breathing steady, I feel the touch of two dry fingers trailing up my leg. I lie perfectly still, eyes closed, and he touches me, no heat in the touch, and then he climbs gently on top of me and I lie perfectly still but soon I have to open my eyes because I'm breathing too hard. The instant I do, he softens, rolls off. When I wake up in the middle of the night, he's gone. His lighter, which looks like a small gold handgun, is on the nightstand next to the empty bottle of wine and the large glass and I remember that when he first showed it to me I thought he was actually going to fire it and when he didn't I felt my life become an anticlimax and looking into his eyes, his gaze rendering everything inconsequential, pools incapable of remembering anything, I moved deeper into them until I was comfortable.

Music from downstairs wakes me at eleven. I hurriedly throw on a robe, walk downstairs, but it's only the maid washing the windows in the den, listening to Culture Club. I say gracias and look outside the window the maid is cleaning and notice that the maid's two young children are swimming in the shallow end of the small pool. I get dressed and wait around the house for Danny to come back. I walk outside, stare at the space where his car was parked, and then I look around for signs of the gardener, who has, for some reason, not shown up in three weeks.

I meet Liz for lunch in Beverly Hills and after we order water I spot William, wearing a beige linen sport jacket, white pleated pants and expensive brown sunglasses, standing at the bar. He makes his way over to our table. I excuse myself and walk to the rest rooms. William follows me and I stand outside the door and ask him what he's doing here and he says that he always comes to this place for lunch and I tell him it's too much of a coincidence and he says, admits, that maybe he talked to Liz, that maybe she had mentioned something to him about lunch with me today at the Bistro Gardens. I tell William that I don't want to see him, that this separation was, inadvertently or not, his idea, that he met Linda. William answers my accusations by telling me that he simply wants to talk and he takes my hand and squeezes it and I pull away and walk back to the table and sit down. William follows and squats by my chair and after he asks me three times to come by his house to talk and I don't say anything he leaves and Liz mumbles apologies and I suddenly, inexplicably, become so hungry that I order two appetizers, a large salad and a bitter-orange tart and eat them quickly, ravenous.

After lunch I walk aimlessly along Rodeo Drive and into Gucci, where I almost buy Danny a wallet, and then I'm walking out of Gucci and leaning against one of the gold columns outside the store in white heat and a helicopter swoops down low out of the sky and back up again and a Mercedes blares its horn at another Mercedes and I remember that I have to do the eleven o'clock edition on Thursdays and I'm shielding my eyes from the sun and I walk into the wrong parking lot and after walking another block find the right one.

I leave the station after the newscast at five ends, telling Jerry that I'll be back for the eleven o'clock edition by ten-thirty and Cliff can do the promos and I get into my car and drive out of the parking lot of the station and find myself driving to the airport, to LAX. I park and walk over to the American Airlines terminal and go to a coffee shop, making sure I get a seat by the window, and I order coffee and watch planes take off, occasionally glancing at a copy of the *L.A. Weekly* I brought with me from the car, and then I do some of the cocaine Simon gave me this afternoon and get diarrhea and then I roam the airport and hope someone will follow me and I walk from one end of the terminal to the other, looking over my shoulder expectantly, and I leave the American Airlines terminal and walk out to the parking lot and approach my car, the windows tinted black, two stubs leaning against the windshield where the wipers used to be, and I get the feeling that there's someone waiting, crouched in the backseat, and I move toward the car, peer in, and though it's hard to tell, I'm pretty sure there's no one in there and I get in and drive out of the airport and as I move past motels that line Century Boulevard leading to LAX I'm tempted, briefly, to check into one of them, just to get the effect, to give off the illusion of being someplace else, and the Go-Go's are singing "Head Over Heels" on the radio and from LAX I drive to West Hollywood and find myself at a revival theater on Beverly Boulevard that's playing an old Robert Altman movie and I park the Jaguar in a towaway zone, pay for a ticket and walk into a small, empty theater, the entire room bathed in red light, and I sit alone up front, flip through the *L.A. Weekly* and it's quiet in the theater except for an Eagles album that's playing somewhere and someone lights a joint and the sweet, strong smell of marijuana distracts me from the *L.A. Weekly*, which drops to the floor anyway after I see an advertisement for Danny's Okie Dog, a hot dog stand on Santa Monica Boulevard, and the lights dim and someone in back yawns and the Eagles fade, a tattered black curtain rises and after the movie ends I walk back outside and get in the car and when the car stalls in front of a gay bar on Santa Monica I decide not to go to the station for the eleven o'clock newscast and I keep turning the key and when the engine starts up again I drive away from the bar and past two young guys yelling at each other in a doorway.

Canter's. I walk into the large, fluorescent-lit delicatessen to get something to eat and buy a pack of cigarettes so that I will have something to do with my hands since I left the *L.A. Weekly* on the floor of the revival theater. I get a booth near the window and study the Benson & Hedges box, then stare out the window and watch streetlights change colors from red to green to yellow to red and nothing passes through the intersection and the lights keep changing and I order a sandwich and a diet Coke and nothing passes, no cars, no people, nothing passes through the intersection for twenty minutes. The sandwich arrives and I stare at it disinterestedly.

A group of punk rockers sit in a booth across from mine and they keep looking over at me, whispering. One of the girls, wearing an old black dress and with short, spiked red hair, nudges the boy sitting next to her and the boy, probably eighteen, lanky and tall, wearing Mack with a blond Mohawk, starts up and walks to my table. The punks suddenly become silent and watch the boy expectantly.

"Um, aren't you on the news or something?" he asks in a high voice that surprises me.

"Yes."

"You're Cheryl Laine, right?" he asks.

"Yes." I look up, trying to smile. "I want to light a cigarette but I don't have matches."

The boy looks at me, made briefly helpless by this last statement, but he recovers and asks, "No matches either but hey, listen, can I have your autograph?" Staring at me hatefully, he says, "I'm, like, your biggest fan." He holds out a napkin and scratches his Mohawk. "You're, like, my favorite anchorperson."

The punks are laughing hysterically. The girl with the red spiked hair covers her pale face with tiny hands and stamps her feet.

"Sure," I say, humiliated. "Do you have a pen?"

He turns around and calls out, "Hey, David, you gotta pen?"

David shakes his head, eyes closed, face contorted with laughter.

"I think I have one," I say, opening my purse. I take a pen out and he hands me a napkin. "What would you like it to say?"

The boy looks at me blankly and then over at the other table and he starts laughing and shrugs. "I don't know."

"Well, what's your name?" I ask, squeezing the pen so tight I'm afraid it will snap. "Let's start there."

"Spaz." He scratches at the Mohawk again.

"Spaz?"

"Yeah. With an *s*."

I write: "To Spaz, best wishes, Cheryl Laine."

"Hey, thanks a lot, Cheryl," Spaz says.

He walks back to the table where the punks are laughing, even harder now. One of the girls takes the autograph from Spaz and looks it over and groans, covering her head with her hands and stamping her feet again.

I very carefully place a twenty-dollar bill on the table and take a sip of the diet Coke and then try, inconspicuously, to get up from the table and I head for the rest room, the punks calling out "Bye, Cheryl" and laughing even louder and once in the ladies' room I lock myself in a stall and lean against a door that's covered with Mexican graffiti and catch my breath. I find Danny's lighter at the bottom of my purse and light a cigarette but it tastes sour and I drop it in the toilet and then walk back through Canter's, which is basically empty, walking all the way around its perimeter, keeping to the rim of the room, avoiding the punks' table and then I'm in my car looking at my reflection in the rearview mirror: eyes red, black smudge on chin, which I try to wipe off. Starting the car, I head for a phone booth on Sunset. I park the car, leaving the engine running, the radio loud, and call my number and I stand in the booth waiting for someone to answer and the phone keeps ringing and I hang up and walk back to the car and drive around, looking for a coffee shop or a gas station so I can use a rest room but everything seems closed and I drive down Hollywood Boulevard looking up at movie marquees and finally I end up getting back on Sunset and driving to Brentwood.

I knock on William's door. It takes him a while to answer it. He asks, "Who's there?" I don't say anything, just knock again.

"Who's there?" he asks, his voice sounding worried.

"It's me," I say, then, "Cheryl."

He unlocks the door and opens it. He's wearing a Polo bathing suit and a T-shirt that has CALIFORNIA written across it in bright-blue letters, a T-shirt I bought him last year, and he has glasses on and doesn't seem surprised to find me standing outside his door.

"I was just going to go in the Jacuzzi," William says.

"I have to use your bathroom," I say quietly. I walk past him and across the living room and into the bathroom. When I come out, William is standing at the bar.

"You couldn't . . . find a bathroom?" he asks.

I sit in a reclining chair in front of a huge television set, ignoring him, then, deciding not to, say, "No."

"Would you like a drink?"

"What time is it?"

"Eleven," he says. "What do you want?"

"Anything."

"I've got pineapple juice, cranberry, orange, papaya."

I had thought he meant alcohol but say, again, "Anything."

He walks over to the TV set and it turns on like a sudden flash, booming, and the news is just beginning and he turns the volume up in time to hear the announcer say: ". . . the Channel Nine news team with Christine Lee filling in for Cheryl Laine . . ." and William walks back to the bar and pours the two of us drinks and he, mercifully, doesn't ask why I'm not there. I turn the television off at the first commercial break.

"Where's Linda?" I ask.

"Palm Springs," he says. "At a colonic seminar." A long, dull silence and then, "Supposedly they're fun."

"That's nice," I murmur. "You two still getting along?"

William smiles and brings me a drink that smells strongly of guava. I sip it cautiously, then put the glass down.

"She just finished redecorating the condo." He motions with his arms and sits down on a beige couch across from the reclining chair. "Even though the condo is temporary." Pause. "She's still at Universal. She's fine." He sips his juice.

William doesn't say anything else. He sips his juice again and then crosses his tan, hairy legs and looks out the window at palm trees lit by streetlamps.

I get up from the chair and walk nervously around the room. I move over to the bookshelf and pretend to look at the titles of the books on the large glass shelf and then at the titles of films on tape in the shelves below.

"You don't look too good," he says. "You have ink on your chin."

"I'm fine."

It takes five minutes for William to say, "Maybe we should have stayed together." He removes his glasses, rubs his eyes.

"Oh God," I say irritably. "No, we shouldn't have stayed together." I turn around. "I knew I shouldn't have come here."

"I was wrong. What can I say?" He looks down at his glasses, then at his knees.

I walk away from the bookshelf and over to the bar and lean against it and there's another long pause and then he asks, "Do you still want me?"

I don't say anything.

"You don't have to answer me, I guess," he says, sounding confused, hopeful.

"This is no use. No, William, I don't." I touch my chin, look at my fingers.

William looks at his drink and before he sips it says, "But you lie all the time."

"Don't call me anymore," I say. "That's why I came over. To tell you this."

"But I think I still"—pause—"want you."

"But I"—I pause awkwardly—"want someone else."

"Does he want you?" he asks with a quiet emphasis, and the fact refuses to escape me untouched and I slump down on a high gray bar-stool.

"Don't crack up," William says. "Don't go to pieces."

"Everything's wrecked."

William gets up from the couch, puts his glass of papaya juice down and carefully walks over to me. He puts a hand on my shoulder, kisses my neck, touches a breast, almost knocking my glass over. I move away to the other side of the room, wiping my face.

"It's surprising to see you like this," I manage to say.

"Why?" William asks from across the room.

"Because you've never felt anything for anybody."

"That isn't true," he says. "What about you?"

"You were never there. You were never there." I stop. "You were never . . . alive."

"I was . . . alive," he says feebly. "Alive?"

"No, you weren't," I say. "You know what I mean."

"What was I, then?" he asks.

"You were just"—I pause, look out over the expanse of white carpet into a massive white kitchen, white chairs on a gleaming tiled floor—"not dead."

"And, uh, this person you're with is?" he asks, an edge in his voice.

"I don't know. He's"—I stammer—"nice. Nice. Good for me."

"He's 'good' for you? What is he? A vitamin? What does that mean? He's good in bed or what?" William raises his arms.

"He can be," I mutter.

"Well, if you met me when I was fifteen—"

"Nineteen," I say, cutting him off.

"Jesus Christ, nineteen," he spits out.

I head for the door, leaving a not unfamiliar scene, and I turn back, once, to look at William and feel a pang of reluctance, which I don't want to feel. I'm imagining Danny, waiting in a bedroom for me, dialing a phone, calling someone, a phantom. Back at my house, the television is on and so is the Betamax. The bed is unmade. A note on top of it reads, "Sorry—I'll see you around. Sheldon called and said he had good news. Set the timer for 11 so the show should be taped. I'm sorry. So long. P.S. Biff thinks you're hot," and below that Biff's phone numbers. The bag of clothes he kept by the bed is gone. Rewinding the tape, I lie down and watch the eleven o'clock edition.

Discovering Japan

HEADING STRAIGHT INTO DARKNESS, staring out the window of a plane at a starless black canvas beyond the window, placing a hand to a window that's so cold it numbs my fingertips and staring at my hand, I withdraw my hand slowly from the window and Roger makes his way down the darkened aisle.

"Set your watch ahead, man," Roger says.

"What, man?" I ask.

"Set your watch ahead. There's a time difference. We're landing in Tokyo." Roger stares at me, his smile slipping. "Tokyo in, um, Japan, okay?" No response, and Roger runs his hand through short blond hair until he's fingering a ponytail in back, sighing.

"But I . . . can't . . . see . . . anything, man," I tell him, slowly pointing to the darkened window.

"That's because you're wearing sunglasses, man," Roger says.

"No, that's not . . . it. It's . . . real"—I think of the right word—"um . . . dark," and then, ". . . man."

Roger looks at me for a minute.

"Well, that's because the windows are, um, tinted," Roger says carefully. "The windows on this plane are tinted, okay?"

I don't say anything.

"Do you want some Valium, a 'lude, some gum, what?" Roger offers.

I shake my head, answer, "No . . . I might OD."

Roger slowly turns around, makes his way up the aisle toward the front of the jet. Pressing my fingertips, still cold from the window, to my forehead causes my eyes to shut tightly.

Naked, waking up bathed in sweat, on a large bed in a suite in the penthouse of the Tokyo Hilton, sheets rumpled on the floor, a young girl nude and sleeping by my side, her head cradled by my arm, which is numb, and it surprises me how much effort it takes to lift it, finally, my elbow brushing carelessly over the girl's face. Clumps of Kleenex that I made her eat, stuck to the sides of her cheeks, her chin, dry, fall off. Turning over, away from the girl, is a boy, sixteen, seventeen, maybe younger, Oriental, nude, on the other side of the bed, arms dangling off the edge, the smooth beige lower back covered with fresh red welts. I reach for a phone by the nightstand but there is no nightstand and the phone is on the floor, disconnected, on top of damp white sheets. Panting, I reach across the boy, connect the phone, which takes about fifteen minutes, finally ask someone on the other end for Roger but Roger, I am told, is at a fruit-eating contest and is not available for comment.

"Get these two kids out of here, okay?" I mumble into the receiver.

I get out of bed, knocking an empty vodka

bottle over onto a bourbon bottle which spills onto potato chip bags and an issue of *Hustler Orient* that this girl on the bed is in this month and I kneel down, open it up, feeling weird while studying how different her pussy looks in the lay-out compared to how it looked three hours ago and when I turn around and look at the bed, the Oriental boy's eyes are open, staring at me. I just stand there, unembarrassed, nude, hungover, and stare back into the boy's black eyes.

"You feel sorry for yourself?" I ask, relieved when two bearded guys open the door and move toward the bed, and I walk into a bathroom and lock the door.

Turning on the bathwater full blast, willing the sound of rushing water hitting the mammoth porcelain tub to drown out the noise of two road-ies dragging the girl and boy out of the bed, out of the room, taking their turn, I lean toward the tub, making sure only cold water pours out of the faucet. I move toward the door, press my ear against it to hear if anybody's still in the room, and pretty sure no one is, I open it, peer out, and nobody's in the room. From a small refrigerator I take out a plastic ice bucket and then move toward the ice machine that was placed at my request in the middle of the suite and get some ice. Then, on my way back to the bathroom, I kneel by the bed and open a drawer and take out a bag of Librium and then I'm back in the bathroom and locking the door and pouring the bucket of ice into the tub, making sure there's enough water at the bottom of the bucket so that I can wash the Librium down my throat, and I step into the tub, lie down, only my head above water, unsettled by the fact that maybe the freezing water and the Librium aren't really such a great combo.

In the dream I'm sitting in the restaurant on top of the hotel near a wall of windows and staring out over the blanket of neon lights that pass for a city. I'm drinking a Kamikaze and sitting across from me is the young Oriental girl from *Hustler* but her smooth brown face is covered with geisha makeup and the geisha makeup and the tight, fluorescent-pink dress and the expression creasing her flat, soft features and the gaze in the blank dark eyes are predatory, making me uneasy, and suddenly the entire blanket of lights flickers, fades, sirens are wailing and people I never noticed are running out of the restaurant, screams, shouts from the black city below, and huge arcs of flame, orange and yellow highlighted against a black sky, shoot up from points on the ground and I'm still staring at the geisha girl, the arcs of flame reflected in her black eyes, and she's mumbling something to me and there's no fear in those large and slanted wet eyes because she's smiling warmly now, saying the same word again and again and again but the sirens and screams and various explosions drown the word out and when I'm shouting, panicked, asking her what she's saying, she just smiles, blinking, and takes out a paper fan and her mouth keeps moving, forming the same word, and I'm leaning toward her to hear the word but a huge claw bursts through the window, showering us with glass, and it grabs me and the claw is warm, pulsing with anger and covered with a slime that drenches the suit I'm wearing and the claw pulls me out the window and I twist toward the girl, who says the word again, this time clearly.

"Godzilla . . . Godzilla, you idiot . . . I said Godzilla . . ."

Screaming silently, I'm lifted toward its mouth, eighty, ninety stories up, looking through what's left of the smashed wall of glass, a cold black wind whipping furiously around me, and the Oriental girl with the pink dress on is now standing on the table, smiling and waving her fan at me, crying out "Sayonara" but it doesn't mean goodbye.

Sometime later, after I climb nude and sobbing from the bathtub, after Roger calls on one of the extensions and tells me that my father has called seven times in the last two hours (something about an emergency), after I tell Roger to tell my father that I'm asleep or out or anything or in another country, after I smash three champagne bottles against one of the walls in the suite, I'm finally able to sit in a chair I've moved over to a window and look out over Tokyo. I'm holding a guitar, trying to write a song, because for the past week a number of chord progressions have been repeating themselves in my head but I'm having a hard time sorting them out and then I'm playing old songs I wrote when I was playing with the band and then I stare at broken glass on the floor that surrounds the bed, thinking: that's a cool album cover. Then I'm picking up a half-empty package of M&M's and washing them down with some vodka and then since it makes me sick I have to head for the bathroom but I trip over the telephone cord and my hand slams into a thick piece of champagne-bottle glass and for a long time I'm staring at my palm, at a thin rivulet of blood racing down my wrist. Unable to shake the glass out, I pull it out and the hole in my hand looks soft and safe and I take the jagged stained piece of glass that still has part of a Dom Perignon label on it and seal the wound by placing it back into it where it looks complete, but the glass falls out and streaming blood covers the guitar I'm beginning to strum and the bloodied guitar will make a pretty good record cover too and I'm able to light a cigarette, blood soaking it only a little. More Librium and I'm asleep but the bed shakes and the earth moving is part of my dream, another monster approaching.

The phone starts ringing at what I can only guess is noon.

"Yeah?" I ask, eyes closed.

"It's me," Roger says.

"I'm sleeping, Lucifer."

"Come on, get up. You're having lunch with someone today."

"Who?'

"Someone," Roger says, irritated. "Come on, let's play."

"I need, like, something," I mumble, opening

my eyes, the sheets, the guitar next to the sheets, covered with brown dried blood, some of it in patches so thick it moves me to open my mouth, then swallow. “I need something, man.”

“What?” Roger's saying. Your Mr. Potato Head broke? What?”

“No, a doctor, man.”

“Why?” Roger sighs.

“Cut my hand.”

“Really?” Roger sounds bored.

“It was bleeding, um, pretty bad.”

“Oh, I'm sure it was. How did you do this?” Roger asks. “In other words: did you have help?”

“I did it shaving—who the fuck cares? Just . . . get a doctor.”

After a while, Roger asks, “If it's not bleeding anymore, does it matter?”

“But there was a lot of . . . blood, man.”

“But does it even hurt?” Roger asks. “Can you even feel it?”

A long pause, then, “No, um, not really.” I wait a minute before saying, “Sort of.”

"I'll get you a doctor. Jesus."

"And a maid. A vacuum. I need a . . . vacuum, man."

"You *are* a vacuum, Bryan," Roger says. I can hear giggling in the background, which Roger silences by hissing, then he tells me, "Your father keeps calling." I can hear Roger lighting a cigarette. "For what it's worth."

"My fingers, um, Roger, won't move."

"Did you hear me or, like, what's the bloody story?"

"What did he want? Is that what you want me to ask?" I sigh. "How did he know where I am?"

"I don't know. Some emergency. Your mom's in the hospital? I'm not sure. Who knows?"

I try to sit up, then with my left hand light a cigarette. When it becomes apparent to Roger that I'm not going to say anything else, Roger says, "I'll give you three hours to get cleaned up. Do you need longer? I hope to holy Christ *not*, okay?"

"Yeah."

"And wear something with long sleeves," Roger warns.

"What?" I ask, confused.

"Long sleeves, man. Wear long sleeves. Something poofy."

I look down at my arms. "Why?"

"Multiple choice: *(a)* you look nice in long sleeves; *(b)* you have holes in your arms; *(c)* you have holes in your arms; *(d)* you have holes in your arms."

A long pause that I finally break up by saying, "*C*?"

"Good," Roger says, then hangs up.

A producer from Warner Brothers who is in Tokyo to meet with Japanese representatives from Sony is thirty and balding and has a face like a death mask and is wearing a kimono with tennis shoes, pacing languidly around his suite, smoking a joint, and it's all really fab and to die over and Roger is flipping through *Billboard*, sitting on a giant unmade bed, and the producer has been on the phone forever and whenever he is put on hold he points at Roger and says, basically, "That mini-pony is really nifty," and Roger, pleased that the producer has noticed the small tuft of hair, nods, turns around, shows the thing off.

"Like Adam Ant?" the producer asks.

"You bet." Roger, who should be mortified, turns back to *Billboard*.

"Help yourself to sake."

Roger leads me by the hand out to the balcony, where two Oriental girls, maybe fifteen, fourteen, sit at a table piled with plates of sushi and what looks like waffles.

"Wow," I say. "Waffles."

"Please don't feel like you're saying too much," Roger says.

"Why don't you just ignore me?" I plead.

"On second thought," Roger says, making a terrible face, "why don't you just sit this one out?"

One of the Oriental girls is wearing pink satin underwear and no top and she's the one I was with last night and the other girl, wearing a police T-shirt, has a Walkman on and glazed eyes. The producer moves over to the balcony doors and is now talking to Manuel about having some deli but no pickles and it's really fab. He clicks off, snaps his fingers as he sits down with a pained expression, motioning for the girl with pink satin underwear to cover herself. The girl, who has a heart of ice, stands up, walks slowly back into the room, turns the television on and falls to the floor with a thump.

The producer sits next to the Oriental girl with the Walkman, sighs, takes a hit off the joint. He offers it to Roger, who shakes his head, then to me. Roger shakes his head for me too.

"Sake?" the producer asks. "It's chilled."

"Great," Roger says.

"Bryan?" the producer asks.

Roger shakes his head again.

"Anybody feel the earthquake?" the producer asks, pouring the sake straight from the bottle into champagne glasses.

"Yeah, I did," Roger says, lighting a cigarette. "Really terrifying," and then, after glancing over at me, "Well, not so scary."

"Don't trust these fucking Japs," the producer says. "I hope it got some of them."

"Who does, man?" Roger sighs, nodding tiredly in agreement.

"They're building an artificial ocean," the producer says. "Several, in fact."

I adjust my sunglasses, look at my hands. Roger readjusts my sunglasses. This moves the producer to get down to business.

He begins gravely. "An idea for a movie. It's actually an idea that has been halfway realized. It is, as we speak, sitting in a vault being guarded by some of the most dangerous men at Warners." Pause. "You're sensing it's a really hot property." Pause. "The reason we came to you, Bryan, is because there are people who remember how intense that movie turned out about the life of the band." His voice gets high and trails off and he studies my face for a reaction, a tough job.

"I mean, holy Jesus, the four of you guys—Sam, Matt and . . ." The producer stops, snaps his fingers, looks at Roger for help.

"Ed," Roger says. "His name was Ed." Pause. "Actually, at the time the band formed it was Tabasco." Pause. "We changed it."

"Ed, gosh," the producer says, pausing awkwardly with such a false reverence that it almost moves me to tears. "What is known as a 'real tragedy.' A real shame. Real upsetting too, I bet, no?"

Roger sighs, nods. "They were already broken up by then."

The producer takes a huge toke off the joint and while inhaling manages to say the following: "You guys were probably one of the pioneering forces in rock during the last decade and it's a shame you broke up—can I interest you in some waffles?"

Roger delicately sips sake, says, "It is a shame," and then looks at me. "Right?"

I sigh. "Sí, señor."

"Since the flick turned out to be so cool and profitable without exploiting anyone, we thought that, um, with your"—the producer glances at Roger for help, falters—"presence, you'd be interested and thrilled to actually star in a movie."

"We receive so many scripts," Roger sighs, adding, "Bryan turned down *Amadeus*, so he's got rather high standards."

"The movie," the producer continues, "is basically the rock-star-in-outer-space thing. An alien creature, this E.T., sabotages the—"

I clutch Roger's arm.

"E.T. An extraterrestrial," Roger says softly.

I let go. The producer continues.

"The E.T. sabotages the dude's limo after a gig at the Forum and after a rather large and fiery chase takes him to this planet where the rock star is held captive. I mean, yadda whatever and there's a princess, who is basically a love interest." The producer pauses, looks at Roger hopefully. "We're thinking Pat Benatar. We're thinking a Go-Go."

Roger laughs. "Oh, that's bloody great."

"The only way the guy can get released is to record songs and perform a concert for the planet's emperor, who is basically a, um, tomato." The producer grimaces, shuddering, then looks worriedly at Roger.

Roger is squeezing the bridge of his nose and saying, "So it's madcap, right?"

"It's *not* tacky and you have a copy," the producer tells Roger. "And everyone is getting excited by the thing in the vault."

Roger smiles, nods, looks over at the Oriental girl and sticks his tongue out, winking. He tells the producer, "I'm not bored."

I actually remember the movie that was made about the band and the movie had gotten it pretty much right except the filmmakers forgot to add the endless paternity suits, the time I broke Kenny's arm, dear liquid in a syringe, Matt crying for hours, the eyes of fans and "vitamins," the look on Nina's face when she demanded a new

Porsche, Sam's reaction when I told him Roger wanted me to do a solo record—information the filmmakers seemed to not want to deal with. The filmmakers seemed to have edited out the time I came home and found Nina sitting in the bedroom in the house on the beach, a pair of scissors in her hand, and they cut out the shot of a punctured, leaking water bed. The editor seemed to have misplaced the scene where Nina tried to drown herself one night at a party in Malibu and they cut the sequence that followed where her stomach was pumped and also the next shot, where she leaned into the frame next to my face and said, "I hate you," and she turned her face, pale and swollen, her hair still wet and plastered to her cheeks, away from me. The movie had been made before Ed jumped from the roof of the Clift Hotel in San Francisco so the filmmakers had an excuse for that scene not being in the movie but there seemed to be no excuse for the rest to have been omitted and for the movie's being made up of bones, an X ray, a set of dull facts, that became wildly popular.

A green lantern hanging from a rafter that shields the balcony pulls me back into the conversation: percentage points, script approval, gross against net profits, terms that, even now, I still find strangely unfamiliar, and I'm staring into Roger's flute of sake and the Oriental girl, inside, is writhing, kicking at the floor, moving in circles, sobbing, and the producer stands up, still talking to Roger, closes the door and smiles when I say, "I'm grateful."

I call Matt. It takes the operator a swift seven minutes to connect me to the number. Matt's fourth wife, Ursula, answers, sighing when I tell her who it is. I wait five minutes for her to come back and I'm imagining Matt standing next to Ursula in the kitchen of a house in Woodland Hills, head bowed down. Instead Ursula says, "He's here," and Matt's voice comes over the line.

"Bryan?"

"Yeah, man, it's me."

Matt whistles. "Whoa." Long pause. "Where are you?"

"Japan. Tokyo, I think."

"Has it been . . . two, three years?"

"No, man, it hasn't been . . . that long," I say. "I don't know."

"Well, man, I heard you were, um, touring."

"World Tour '84, man."

"I heard something about that . . ." His voice trails off.

Tense, awkward silence broken only by "yeah"s and "um"s.

"I saw the video," he says.

"The one with Rebecca De Mornay?"

"Er, no, the one with the monkey."

"Oh . . . yeah."

"I heard the album," Matt finally says.

"Did . . . you like it, man?" I ask.

"Are you kidding, man?" he says.

"Is that . . . good, man?" I ask.

"Great backup. Really tight."

Another long silence.

"It's, um, valid, man, valid," Matt says. Pause. "The one about the car, man?" Pause. "I saw John Travolta buy a copy at Tower." Long pause.

"I'm, um, really gratified by your response, man," I say. "Okay?"

Long pause.

"Are you, um, doing anything, like, now?" I ask.

"I've fooled around with some stuff," Matt says. "Might be ready to go into the studio in a couple of months."

"Ter-rif-ic," I say.

"Uh-huh."

"Have you . . . talked to Sam?" I ask.

"Just about . . . well, maybe it was a month ago? One of the lawyers? Ran into him somewhere. By accident."

"Sam is . . . okay?"

Not sounding too sure, Matt says, "He's great."

"And . . . his lawyers?"

He answers by asking, "How's Roger?"

"Roger is . . . Roger."

"Out of rehab?"

"A long time ago."

"Yeah, I know what you mean." Matt sighs. "I know what you mean, man."

"Well, man." I breathe in, tense up. "I wonder if maybe you'd like to, oh I don't know, if maybe you would like to get together and write some songs when I get finished with this tour, maybe record some stuff . . . man?"

Matt coughs, then after not too long says, "Oh man I don't know y'know the old days are over man and I really don't think so."

"Well, fuck, it's not like—" I stop in mid-sentence.

"You gotta move on."

"I . . . I am, you know, but." I start to kick my foot against a wall and my fingernails have somehow dug themselves so hard into the bandaged wound that it becomes spotted with red.

"It's over, y'know, man?" Matt is saying.

"Am I, like, lying, man?"

I'm not saying anything, just blowing on my palm.

"I was watching some of those old movies that Nina and Dawn took in Monterey," Matt is saying.

I'm trying not to listen, thinking *Dawn?*

"And the weirdest thing but also the grooviest thing is that Ed looked really good. He looked great, in fact. Tan and in good shape and I don't know what happened." Pause. "I don't know what the fuck happened, man."

"Who cares, man?"

"Yeah." Matt sighs. "You've got a point."

"Because I don't care, man."

"I guess I don't care either, man."

I hang up, pass out.

On the way to the arena, sitting in the back of the limo, watching television, sumo wrestling, what could be an old Bruce Lee movie, the same commercial about a blue lemonade seven times, throwing ice cubes I've sucked on at the small square screen, I roll the glass partition down and tell the chauffeur I need a lot of cigarettes and the chauffeur reaches into the glove compartment, tosses back a pack of Marlboros, and the cocaine I'd taken earlier isn't doing much of anything, which I expected, and dismayingly it just seems to intensify the pain in my hand and I keep swallowing but residue keeps tickling the back of my throat in an insistent, annoying kind of way and I keep drinking Scotch which almost takes away the taste.

The stage reeks of sweat and it's a hundred degrees onstage and we have been playing for about fifty minutes and all I want to do is sing the last song, which the band, when I mention this in between breaks, thinks is a pretty bad idea. All the songs are from the last three solo albums but from the front row I can hear Orientals crying out in thick, *r*-less accents the names of big hits I played with the band and this band launches into the biggest hit off the second solo LP and I can't really tell if the audience is enthused even when they applaud loudly and behind me a four-hundred-foot tapestry—BRYAN METRO WORLD TOUR 1984—billows in back of us and I'm moving slowly across the large expanse of stage, trying to peer out into the audience but bright blinding spotlights turn the arena into this moving mass of gray darkness and as I begin to sing the second verse of the song I forget the lyrics. I sing "Another night passes by and still you wonder what happened" and then I freeze. A guitarist suddenly jerks his head up and a bassist moves closer toward me, the drummer still keeping beat. I'm not even playing my guitar anymore. I start the second verse again: "Another night passes by and still you wonder what happened . . .," then nothing. The bassist yells out something. I turn my head toward him, my hands killing me, and the bassist urges "You give the world one more try" and I'm saying "What?" and the bassist calls out "You give the world one more try" and I'm saying "What?" and the bassist yells "You give the world one more try—Jesus" and I'm thinking to myself why in the hell would I sing this and then who the fuck wrote this piece of shit and I motion for the band to go into the chorus and we finish the song okay and there's no encore.

Roger rides with me in the limo back to the hotel.

"Terrific show, Bryan." Roger sighs. "Your concentration and showmanship really cannot be improved upon. I would be lying if I said they could. I'm all out of superlatives."

"My hands are . . . fucked up."

"Just the hands?" he says, not even really sarcastically, no edge in his voice, a muffled complaint maybe, an observation not worth making. "We'll just tell the promoters you had an uneven synth mix," Roger says. "We'll just tell people that your mother died."

We pass a crowded street diagonal to the hotel and everyone is trying to peer into the tinted windows as the limo rolls toward the Hilton.

"Jesus," I'm mumbling to myself. "All these fucking gooks. Just look at them, Roger. Just look at all these fucking gooks, Roger."

"All those fucking gooks bought your last album," Roger says, then adds, under his breath, "You brain-dead asshole."

I'm sighing, putting my sunglasses on. "I'd like to get out of this limo and tell these gooks what I think of them."

"That's not gonna happen, baby."

"Why . . . not?"

"Because you aren't presentable for direct contact with the public."

"Think of all the words that rhyme with my name, Roger," I say.

"Are there a lot?" Roger asks.

Roger and I are standing in an elevator.

"Get me a maid or something, okay?" I ask him. "My room is like a total wreck, man."

"Clean it yourself."

"No. Unh-uh."

"I'll move you, okay?"

"Okay."

"You've got the whole floor, you cadaver. Take your pick."

"Why can't you just get me a maid?"

"Because housekeeping at the Tokyo Hilton seems to think that you raped two of their maids. Is this true, Bryan?"

"Define, um, rape, Roger."

"I'll have room service send up a dictionary." Roger makes a terrible face.

"I'm going to move."

Roger sighs, looks at me and says, "You're getting the feeling that you're not going to move, right? You're realizing that you were going to consider it but now you're coming to the conclusion that it would not be worth the effort, that you don't have the strength or something, right?" Roger turns away, the elevator gradually slowing, reaching his floor. Roger turns a key so that the elevator is locked into going to my floor and not anywhere else, like I even want it to.

The elevator stops at the floor that Roger has put a lock on and I step into an empty, dim-lit corridor and start walking toward my door, breaking the hush by screaming loudly, twice, three, four times, and I fumble for the key that will open the door and I turn the handle and it's open anyway and inside is a young girl sitting on my bed, dried blood everywhere, leafing through *Hustler*. She looks up from the magazine. I close the door, lock it, stare at her.

"Was that you screaming?" the girl asks in a small, tired voice.

"Guess," I say and then, "Have you made friends with the ice machine yet?"

The girl is pretty, blond, dark tan, large wide

blue eyes, Californian, a T-shirt with my name on it, faded tight cutoff jeans. Her lips are red, shiny, and she puts the magazine down as I slowly move toward her, almost tripping over a used dildo that Roger calls The Enabler. She stares back, nervously, but the way she gets up off the bed, walking slowly backward, seems too calculated and when she finally hits the wall and stands there breathing hard and I reach her, I have to put my hands around her neck, softly at first, then tightening the grip, and she shuts her eyes and I bring her toward me then slam her head against the wall which doesn't seem to faze her and this worries me, until she opens her eyes and grins and in one swift movement lifts her hand, the fingernails long and sharp and pink, and rips a two-hundred-dollar T-shirt down the front, scratching my chest. I bunch my fist and hit her hard. She claws at my face. I push her down on the floor and she's spitting at me, plugging my mouth with her fingers, squealing.

I'm in the bathtub taking a bubble bath. The girl has lost a tooth and is nude and sitting on the toilet seat, holding an ice pack from room service (who left several) up to the side of her face. She stands unsteadily and limps over to the mirror and says, "I think the swelling's gone down." I pick up a piece of ice that floats in the water and put it in my mouth and chew it, concentrating on how slowly I am chewing. She sits back down on the toilet and sighs.

"Don't you want to know where I'm from?" she asks.

"No," I say. "Not really."

"Nebraska. Lincoln, Nebraska." A long pause.

"You had a job at the mall, right?" I ask, eyes closed. "But the mall closed down, right? It's all empty now, huh?"

I can hear her light a cigarette, smell its smoke, then ask, "Have you been there?"

"I've been to a mall in Nebraska," I say.

"Yeah?"

"Yeah."

"It's all flat."

"Flat," I agree.

"Totally."

"Totally flat."

I stare down at torn skin on my chest, at the pink swollen lines that crisscross the skin below, over my nipples and I'm thinking, There goes another photo shoot without a shirt on. I touch the nipples lightly, brush the girl's hand away when she tries to touch them. Once she's properly lubricated I slide into her again.

A gram and I'm ready to call Nina at the house up in Malibu. The phone rings eighteen times. She finally answers.

"Hello?"

"Nina?"

"Yeah?"

"It's me."

"Oh." Pause. "Wait a minute." Another pause. "Are you there?"

"You sound like you care," she says.

"Maybe I do, babe."

"Maybe you don't, asshole."

"Jesus."

"I'm fine," she says quickly. "Where are you now?"

I close my eyes, lean up against the headboard. "Tokyo. A Hilton."

"Sounds classy."

"It is far and away the nicest place I have ever lived."

"That's great."

"You don't sound too enthusiastic, babe."

"Yeah?"

"Oh shit. Just let me talk to Kenny."

"He's on the beach with Martin."

"Martin?" I ask, confused. "Who the hell is Martin?"

"Marty, Marty, Marty, Marty—"

"Okay, okay, yeah, Marty. How's Marty?"

"Marty's great."

"Yeah? That's great, even though I have no idea who he is, but, um, can I talk to Kenny, babe?" I ask. "I mean, can you go out to the beach and get him and not like freak out?"

"Some other time, okay?"

"I would like to talk to my kid."

"But he doesn't want to talk to you."

"Let me talk to my kid, Nina." I sigh.

"This is pointless," she says.

"Nina—just go get Kenny."

"I'm going to hang up on you now, okay, Bryan?"

"Nina, I'll get my lawyer."

"Fuck your lawyer, Bryan, just fuck him. I've gotta go."

"Oh Jesus—"

"And it's not a good idea if you call here too often."

A long silence because I don't say anything.

"It is never a good idea if you talk to Kenny, because you scare him," she says.

"And you don't?" I ask, appalled. "Medusa?"

"Never call back." She hangs up.

Sitting in the empty coffee shop (which Roger had "cordoned off" because he was afraid "people would see you") in the bottom of the Tokyo Hilton, Roger tells me that we are going to be watching the English Prices eat lunch. Roger is wearing huge black sunglasses and an expensive pair of pajamas, chewing bubble gum.

"Who?" I ask. "*Who?*"

"The English Prices," Roger enunciates clearly, again. "New group. MTV discovered them and has made them big." Pause. "Real big," he adds grimly. "They're from Anaheim."

"Why?" I ask.

"Because-they-were-born-there." Roger sighs.

"Uh-huh," I say.

"They want to meet you."

"But . . . why?"

"Good question," Roger says. "But does it really matter to you?"

"Why are they here?"

"Because they are on tour," Roger says. "Are you doing coke?"

"Grams and grams and grams of it," I say. "If you knew how much you would choke."

"I suppose it's better than the angel dust routine from '82." Roger sighs warily.

"Who are these people, Roger?" I ask.

"Who are you?"

"Um . . .," I say, confused by this question. "Who . . . do you think?"

"Someone who tried to set his ex-wife on fire with a tiki torch?" he suggests.

"I was married to her then."

"I suppose it was a good thing that Nina threw herself in the ocean." Roger pauses. "Of course it was three months later, but considering how smart she was when you first met, I was glad her reflexes had improved." Roger lights a cigarette, thinks everything over. "Christ, I can't believe she got custody. But then I hate to think what would've happened to that kid if you had gotten custody. Mothra would have made a better parent."

"Roger, who are these people?"

"Have you seen the cover of the new *Rolling Stone*?" Roger asks, snapping his fingers at a young, nervous Oriental waitress. "Oh, I forgot. You don't read that publication anymore."

"Not after that shit they pulled with Ed's death."

"Touchy, touchy." Roger sighs. "The English Prices are hot. A hot album, *Toadstool*, and a video game made about them that you should play, er, sometime." Roger points to his coffee cup and the waitress, head bowed dutifully, pours. "It sounds tacky but it's not. Really."

"Jesus, I'm a wreck."

"The English Prices are big," Roger reminds me. "Stratosphere isn't an inappropriate word."

"You said that already and I still don't believe you."

"Just be cool."

"Why the fuck do I have to be cool?" I look

straight at Roger for the first time since we entered the coffee shop.

Roger looks down at his cup and then at me and enunciates each word very carefully: "Because I am going to be managing them."

I don't say anything.

"They'll bring in a lot more people," Roger says. "A *lot* more people."

"For what? For who?" I ask, instantly realizing the question is useless, better left unanswered.

"For you, babes," Roger says. "We've been drawing sizable crowds, but still."

"There isn't gonna be another tour, man," I say. "This is it."

"That's what you think, baby," Roger says casually.

"Oh man," is all I say.

Roger looks up. "Oh shit—here the little bastards come. Just be cool."

"Jesus fucking Christ." I sigh. "I *am* cool."

"Just keep telling yourself that and roll your sleeves down."

"I am becoming aware of just how lost inside my life you really are," I say, rolling my sleeves down.

Four members of the English Prices walk into the coffee shop and each of them has a young Oriental girl by his side. The Oriental girls are very young and pretty and wearing striped miniskirts and T-shirts and pink leather boots. The lead singer of the English Prices is very young also, younger than the Oriental girls in fact, and he has a short platinum-blond burr of hair on his head and smooth tan skin and he's wearing mascara and red eyeliner and is dressed in black leather and has a spiked bracelet wrapped around the wrist he holds out. We shake hands.

"Hey, man, I've been a fan of yours like forever," I hear him say. "Forever, man."

The other members nod their heads sullenly in agreement. It's impossible for me to smile or nod. We're all sitting at a large glass table and the Oriental girls keep staring at me, giggling.

"Where's Gus?" Roger asks.

"Gus has mono." The lead singer turns to Roger, eyes still on me.

"I'll have to send him some flowers," Roger says.

The singer turns back to me, explains, "Gus is our drummer."

"Oh," I say. "That's . . . nice."

"Sushi?" Roger asks them.

"No, I'm a vegetarian," the singer says. "Plus we already had a big breakfast of SpaghettiOs."

"With who?"

"A big important record executive."

"Hip," Roger says.

"Anyway, man," the lead singer says, turning his full attention back to me. "like, I was listening to your records—well, the band's records—since I can remember. In, like, well, a long time ago, and I'm not guessing when I tell you that you"—he stops and has trouble pronouncing the next word—". . . influenced us."

The rest of the English Prices nod, mumbling in unison.

I try to look the singer in the eyes. I try to say "Great." No one says anything.

"Hey," the lead singer says to Roger. "He's pretty, uh, subdued."

"Yes," Roger says. "We call him, in fact, Sub Dude."

"That's . . . cool," the lead singer says apprehensively.

"Who were you listening to, man?" one of them asks me.

"When?" I ask, confused.

"In, like, when you were a little kid, in, like, high school and stuff. Influences, man."

"Oh . . . lots of things. Um, I don't really remember . . ." I look at Roger for help. "I'd prefer not to say."

"Do you want me to, like, repeat the question, man?" the lead singer asks.

I just stare at him, frozen, unable to move.

"That's life," the lead singer finally says, sighing.

"Captain Beefheart, the Ronettes, antiestablishment rage, you know," Roger says blithely, then, "Who are your friends?" He laughs slyly and the lead singer laughs, barking, and that's the cue for the rest of the band to follow.

"These girls are great."

"Yes sir," one of them says in a deep monotone with a lisp. "Can't understand one bit of American but they fuck like rabbits."

"Can't you?" the lead singer asks the girl sitting next to him. "You a good fuck, bitch?" he asks, a sincere expression on his face, nodding. The girl looks at the expression, takes in the nod, the smile, and she smiles back a worried, innocent smile and nods and everyone laughs.

The lead singer, nodding and smiling, asks another girl, "You give real good head, right? You like it when I slap your face with my fat leathery cock, you gook bitch?"

The girl nods, smiling, looks at the other girls, and the band laughs, Roger laughs, the Oriental girls laugh. I laugh, finally taking off my sunglasses, loosening up a little. Silence takes over and everyone at the table is left, momentarily, to his own uneasy devices. Roger tells the band to order some drinks. The Oriental girls giggle, adjust tiny pink boots, the lead singer keeps glancing at my bandaged hand and I see myself in the same naive curled grin, in the blur of a photo session, in a hotel room in San Francisco, in a zillion dollars, in another ten months.

In a dressing room at the arena before we are supposed to go on, I just sit in a chair in front of a huge oval mirror staring at my reflection through Wayfarers, at myself nibbling radishes. I start to kick my foot against the wall, my fists clenched. Roger walks in, sits down, lights a cigarette. After a while I say something.

"What?" Roger asks. "You're mumbling."

"I don't want to go out there."

"Because why?" Roger asks as if speaking to a child.

"I don't feel too good." I stare at my reflection, uselessly.

"Don't say that. You have a distinctly upbeat air about you."

"Yeah, and you're gonna win Mr. Congeniality any fucking year now," I growl, then, calmed down, "Get Reggie."

"Get ready for what?" he asks and then, seeing that I am about to pounce on him, relents. "Just a joke."

Roger makes a phone call, ten minutes later someone is wrapping something around my arm, a vein is slapped, pinpricks, vitamins, saying yeah, weird warmness rushing through me, flushing out the coldness, fast at first, then, more slowly, yeah, sure.

Roger sits back down on the couch and says, "Don't beat up any more groupies, all right? Can you hear me? *Lay* off."

"Oh man," I say. "They . . . like . . . it. They like to pet me. I let them pet . . . me."

"Just *cool* it. Do you hear me?"

"Oh man fuck you man I'll do it again."

"What did you say to me?"

"Man, I'm Bryan—"

"I know who you are," Roger cuts me off. "You're the same awful asshole who beat up three girls on the last tour, threatened one with a carving knife. These are girls we are still paying off. Do you remember that bitch from Missouri?"

"Missouri?" I giggle.

"The one you almost killed?" Roger says. "Does that refresh your memory?"

"No."

"We are still paying her and some scumbag lawyer off—"

"You're getting heavy, man, and when you're getting heavy . . . you must, um, leave me alone."

"Do you remember how you fucked that one up?"

"Don't dwell on the past, dude."

"Do you know how much we still have to pay that bitch off every fucking *month*?"

"Leave me alone," I whisper.